MESSENGER

THE LEGEND OF JOAN OF ARC

MESSENGER
THE LEGEND OF JOAN OF ARC
A GRAPHIC NOVEL

WRITTEN BY
TONY LEE

ILLUSTRATED BY
SAM HART

COLORED BY
SAM HART with **FLAVIO COSTA**

LETTERED BY
CADU SIMÕES

CANDLEWICK PRESS

The Hundred Years' War — in which France and England fought for the ever-changing French throne.

One hundred sixteen years of fighting, with small patches of peace. Generations lived and died knowing nothing else.

But then came the prophet, the messenger from God. The French began to fight back, scaring the English and forcing their allies to put her on trial for heresy....

...AND I WILL NOT REVEAL THOSE TO SAVE MY HEAD.

ORDER! ORDER, I TELL YOU!

AS YOU WISH. LET US MOVE ON. YOUR *CLOTHES*, CHILD.

DO YOU NOT FIND THAT A GIRL WEARING *MEN'S CLOTHING* TO TRIAL IS OF POOR TASTE?

THIS IS WHAT THE GUARDS *GAVE* ME. IF I HAD A DRESS, I WOULD WEAR IT.

OR WOULD THAT *HURT* YOUR CASE AGAINST ME? AFTER ALL, YOU CLAIM THAT A *WOMAN WEARING MEN'S CLOTHES* IS AGAINST GOD'S DECREE!

YOU'D RATHER WEAR MEN'S CLOTHING, *WOULDN'T YOU?* EASIER TO TRY TO *ESCAPE* AGAIN!

PLEASE, TRY— BECAUSE *ESCAPING FROM YOUR PENANCE* WOULD HAVE YOU *AUTOMATICALLY* CONVICTED OF HERESY *AS WELL!*

I DON'T RECOGNIZE YOUR *AUTHORITY*, BISHOP— YOU HELP THE *BURGUNDIANS*, OUR *ENEMIES*, WHO ARE ALLIED WITH *ENGLAND!*

AND I PLEDGED *NO OATH* THAT I WOULD NOT ESCAPE FROM MY ENEMIES, SO WHY SHOULDN'T I TRY? WANTING TO ESCAPE ISN'T *HERESY*. IT'S A PART OF BEING IN A *WAR*.

LET US TALK OF YOUR *CHILDHOOD*. BORN IN *DOMRÉMY*, YOU LIVED A NORMAL LIFE, DID YOU NOT?

YOUR FATHER, *JACQUES D'ARC*, WAS A VILLAGE OFFICIAL.

HE WAS A *FARMER*, YES—WE OWNED NEARLY FIFTY ACRES OF LAND.

HE WAS IN CHARGE OF THE LOCAL *MILITIA* AND COLLECTED THE TAXES, AMONG OTHER THINGS.

DOMRÉMY WAS— *IS*—LOYAL TO THE FRENCH, BUT AT THE TIME WAS SURROUNDED BY *BURGUNDIAN* TERRITORY.

WE WERE OFTEN RAIDED, ATTACKED BY BANDITS. ON ONE OCCASION THEY TRIED TO *BURN DOWN OUR VILLAGE*.

SO FROM AN EARLY AGE YOU WERE SURROUNDED BY SOLDIERS, WEAPONS?

FARMERS DEFENDING THEIR LAND AREN'T THE SAME AS *KNIGHTS IN ARMOUR*, BISHOP.

ALTHOUGH AS YOU *NEVER* VISIT THE VILLAGES, I'M NOT SURPRISED YOU *DON'T KNOW* THIS.

HA HA HA HA HA HA

TELL ME MORE ABOUT YOUR *UPBRINGING*. YOU'VE SAID THAT AS A CHILD, YOU WERE TAUGHT *PRAYERS—*

THE *PATERNOSTER, AVE MARIA,* AND *CREDO* AMONG OTHERS.

YES, THAT IS TRUE.

COULD YOU REPEAT THE *PATERNOSTER—*THE *LORD'S PRAYER—*FOR US NOW?

OF COURSE, BISHOP—IT WOULD BE MY PLEASURE.

JUST AS SOON AS YOU HEAR MY *CONFESSION,* WHICH YOU HAVE *AVOIDED* THESE MANY MONTHS PAST.

YOU SEEM TO WANT TO MAKE ME OUT TO BE A WARRIOR FROM BIRTH—OR SOME KIND OF *HERETIC DEVIL CHILD—*BUT I LED A NORMAL LIFE.

AS A YOUNG GIRL I LEARNT TO SPIN AND SEW; I PLAYED AROUND THE *FAIRY TREE* WITH THE OTHER CHILDREN.

I CONFESSED MY SINS ONCE A YEAR...

...AND WHEN I WAS THIRTEEN, I HEARD THE *VOICE OF GOD.*

HERESY!

HERESY!

HERESY!

HERESY!

HERESY!

ORDER! ORDER, I TELL YOU!

YOUR COUNTRY IS IN *PERIL*. FRANCE NEEDS A *MESSENGER FROM GOD*, A PROPHET TO HELP ITS PEOPLE IN THEIR TIME OF NEED.

YOU WILL BE THAT PROPHET.

I DON'T UNDERSTAND WHAT YOU MEAN— AM I TO *JOIN THE CHURCH*?

NO, YOU WILL BE *FAR MORE*. YOU WILL BE A BRIGHT *FLAME OF FAITH*, SHINING AGAINST THE DARKNESS.

YOU WILL *UNITE FRANCE* AGAINST AN ENEMY— AND REGAIN A *CROWN* FOR A KING.

BUT THE BRIGHTEST FLAMES *BURN OUT FASTEST*.

YOUR LIFE WILL BE A *SHORT* ONE. YOU WILL NEVER MARRY OR HAVE CHILDREN—IT WILL BE A LIFE OF *HARDSHIP AND SCORN*.

BUT YOU WILL END IT BY *GOD'S SIDE*, EMBRACED BY *ANGELS*.

JEHANNE! ARE YOU ALL RIGHT? ARE YOU HURT?

I AM *FINE*, DURAND—JUST SCRATCHES AND BRUISES...

...BUT I FEAR I WILL *NEVER* BE THE SAME AGAIN.

YOUR COUSIN *WORRIES* US WITH NEWS OF YOUR ACCIDENT. ARE YOU SURE YOU'RE NOT HURT, JEHANNE?

I'M FINE, FATHER. THE *ANGEL* MADE ME BETTER, ANYWAY!

ANGEL?

WELL, MORE OF A *SAINT*, REALLY. MICHAEL. HE CAME WITH WORDS FROM *GOD*.

I'M GOING TO BE A *MESSENGER*. HE TOLD ME THINGS ABOUT MY FUTURE.

YOU DON'T FEEL *FEVERISH*, YET YOU'RE *DELIRIOUS*!

NOT AT ALL, MOTHER! GOD WILL *GUIDE* ME—EVERYTHING WILL BE OK!

I UNDERSTAND MY *ROLE* NOW.

ENOUGH!

JEHANNE, TO SPEAK THIS WAY ABOUT THE LORD IS *HERESY*. ONLY THE *POPE IN ROME* TALKS TO GOD! CHILD OR NO CHILD, YOU COULD BE *BURNT AT THE STAKE* FOR IT. IT'S NOTHING MORE THAN *WITCHCRAFT*!

I AM RESPONSIBLE FOR THE DEFENCE OF THIS VILLAGE, AND I CANNOT HAVE A DAUGHTER THAT IS BELIEVED TO BE *DEVIL-TOUCHED*!

YOU MUST BE CONCUSSED. YOU WILL STAY IN BED UNTIL YOU ARE WELL AGAIN. UNTIL THESE "VOICES" ARE *GONE*.

A WEEK LATER.

JEHANNE! WHAT ARE YOU *DOING*? YOUR FATHER WILL KILL YOU IF HE CATCHES YOU *DISOBEYING* HIM!

I DON'T CARE WHAT FATHER SAYS! MICHAEL CAME TO ME, DURAND! THERE'S A *LAMB TRAPPED*, AND SAVING HIM WILL LEAD TO BIGGER THINGS!

I'M SORRY, DURAND, BUT I *HAVE* TO DO THIS!

COME ON, WHERE ARE YOU?

BAAA!!!

THERE YOU ARE. STAY STILL; I'LL FREE YOU IN A MOMENT.

HOW DID YOU KNOW THE LAMB WAS *HERE*, JEHANNE? COULD YOU HEAR IT?

NO...IT WAS TOO FAR AWAY... DURAND SAID YOUR *VOICES* TOLD YOU...

PULL BACK! *RETREAT!* THERE ARE NO PICKINGS HERE TODAY!

JUST THE CURSES OF A *GODLESS DEVIL CHILD!*

YEEAAHHH!!!! FLEE, YOU COWARDS!

TO MY DAUGHTER! WHO TURNED AWAY THE BURGUNDIANS WITH NOTHING BUT *WORDS!*

AYE, BUT SHE SHOULDN'T MAKE JOKES ABOUT *HEARING GOD.* THAT COULD GET HER *BURNT AS A WITCH.*

DON'T LISTEN TO HIM, CHILD. I DON'T KNOW HOW YOU DID IT, BUT IT WAS A *MIRACLE.*

AND THE CHURCH DOESN'T BURN PEOPLE WHO PERFORM MIRACLES.

BUT IT *WILL,* FATHER. IT WILL.

A MESSAGE FROM YOUR *SAINTLY FRIENDS*, JEHANNE?

NO, FATHER. FROM LESSONS GIVEN BY A *GOOD TEACHER*.

1427.

YES, SAINT MICHAEL, I *UNDERSTAND*.

I JUST WISH THERE WAS ANOTHER WAY. WHY DOES IT HAVE TO BE *ME*? WHY CAN'T YOU TELL A LORD, OR EVEN THE *POPE HIMSELF*?

THE CONVERSATIONS ARE MORE *FREQUENT* NOW. IT'S ALMOST AS IF SHE'S BEING *PREPARED*.

INDEED, FATHER HUGO. BUT FOR *WHAT*? I HAVE NO IDEA.

I'VE TRIED TO STOP HER, BUT WHAT CAN I DO? NOTHING BUT WATCH HER *WALK TO THE SCAFFOLD* HERSELF WHEN THE CHURCH COMES FOR HER.

1428.

HEY, JEHANNE! COME AND *DANCE* WITH US.

WHAT DID YOU DO *THAT* FOR? WE DON'T WANT *HER KIND* AROUND THE TREE!

SHE'S *DEVIL-TOUCHED*, THAT ONE! TALKS TO *DEMONS*, BUT SHE SAYS IT'S *GOD*!

OW! I JUST THOUGHT I'D BE NICE TO HER.

WE USED TO BE *FRIENDS*!

-SOB-

THANK YOU, LORD.

JEHANNE! JOAN! WHAT *EVER* IS THE *MATTER*, CHILD?

THE SAINTS, THEY'VE *SPOKEN* TO ME, FATHER HUGO.

THEY'VE TOLD ME WHAT I MUST *DO*. THEY'VE SHOWN ME MY PATH.

BUT SURELY THIS IS A *GOOD THING*, MY CHILD?

TO KNOW YOUR PATH, TO HAVE *GOD HIMSELF* GUIDING YOU?

YOU'D *THINK* SO, WOULDN'T YOU? BUT IF IT WERE, THEN THE CHURCH WOULDN'T CALL IT *HERESY*. THEY WOULDN'T *PUNISH* YOU.

GOD SPOKE TO ME. HE TOLD ME THAT I MUST BE HIS *MESSENGER*. THAT I MUST SPEAK FOR HIM.

FIGHT FOR HIM.

DIE FOR HIM.

BUT WHY? WHY WOULD GOD ASK SO MUCH OF *YOU*? YOU'RE JUST A *GIRL*!

I HAVE A MESSAGE FOR THE *DAUPHIN*, FATHER HUGO.

THE WAR AGAINST THE ENGLISH IS GOING *BADLY*. THE BURGUNDIANS ARE ALLIED WITH THEM, AND THE FRENCH ARE *LOSING HOPE*.

I'M TO GUIDE HIS FORCES AGAINST THE *ENGLISH* AND HAVE HIM CROWNED *KING*. ALTHOUGH *HOW* I DO THAT, I HAVE NO IDEA.

THE ENGLISH HOLD *REIMS*, WHERE THE DAUPHIN NEEDS TO BE *CROWNED*. UNTIL IT IS WON BACK, FRANCE WILL *NEVER* HAVE A KING TO LEAD IT.

AND WITHOUT A KING, WE CANNOT HOPE TO *END* THIS WAR.

WELL, IF THIS IS WHAT YOU *BELIEVE*, THEN YOU MUST SPEAK TO THE *DAUPHIN* HIMSELF.

YES, FATHER.

I'LL JUST TRAVEL TO *CHINON* RIGHT NOW AND *ASK FOR AN AUDIENCE*!

YOU REASON WELL, CHILD.

HOWEVER, CHARLES'S FORCES ARE IN *VAUCOU-LEURS*, NOT FAR FROM HERE. PERHAPS THE GARRISON CAPTAIN, *ROBERT DE BAUDRICOURT*, COULD HELP?

OF COURSE! *HE'LL* KNOW THE DAUPHIN! HE COULD WRITE A LETTER OF *INTRODUCTION*.

WE WILL START THERE. *COMING*, FATHER?

I can **stop** this, Father. I can bring an end to the attacks.

All I need to do is speak to the garrison captain at Vaucouleurs; Father Hugo says his name is **Robert de Baudricourt**.

Baudricourt will introduce me to the Dauphin—and Charles will listen to me. He **has** to! And the war will change when he does.

For **four years** you've believed in my voices. Please, believe in them now.

There's a huge difference between having a **lord save a village** and a **king save a country**.

Your **faith** in the voices is admirable, but people won't believe you. They'll think you're mad or—worse—a **heretic**.

So I won't let you go **alone**. Durand, go with your cousin. Ensure she returns safely. By **force** if needs be.

Yes, Uncle.

Thank you, Father!

Yes, yes... Now, go on with you. Save the **village**, save **France**, do whatever you need to do. Just come home safe, you hear?

I'll do my best, Father.

HAHA HAHA!

THANK YOU, CHILD. WE HAVEN'T HAD A GOOD LAUGH IN DAYS!

NOW, LISTEN HERE! MY COUSIN IS A *PROPHET FROM GOD*! SHE HAS SAVED OUR VILLAGE ON MORE THAN ONE OCCASION!

IF GOD SAYS SHE MUST SPEAK TO THE DAUPHIN— THEN *STEP ASIDE*!

YOUR COUSIN IS AN *IDIOT* WHO HEARS VOICES IN THE WIND. WE HAVE A DOZEN LIKE HER *EVERY WEEK*, TELLING US THE WORD OF THE LORD.

WE NEED *SOLDIERS*, NOT *MADWOMEN*. TAKE HER HOME...

...TAKE HER HOME TO HER FATHER AND GIVE HER A GOOD *WHIPPING*.

NOW, LISTEN HERE—

THERE'S NO POINT, MY CHILD. HIS MIND IS CLOSED.

WE'LL FIND *ANOTHER* WAY TO REACH THE DAUPHIN.

I'VE FAILED!

MY *FIRST TASK*, AND I'VE *FAILED*!

1429.

I FAILED, FATHER. THESE PAST *FEW MONTHS* I'VE WRITTEN TO BAUDRICOURT, BUT HE HASN'T REPLIED TO MY LETTERS.

HE IS A MAN OF *ACTION*, MY CHILD. I FEAR WE MUST FIND A MORE *DIRECT* APPROACH.

PERHAPS IF YOU *ASK* FOR SOME ADVICE?

I WILL. BUT THE VOICES HAVE BEEN QUIET OF LATE.

BLESS ME, FATHER—

ARGH!!

YOU HAVE *DISPLEASED* US, CHILD. YOU HAVE *NOT SAVED FRANCE.* YOU HAVE STAYED AT HOME AND DONE *NOTHING.*

—HNF— I AM A POOR GIRL. I DO NOT KNOW HOW TO RIDE OR FIGHT!

ALL YOU NEED TO DO IS SPEAK TO THE *DAUPHIN.*

HIS *SCOTTISH ALLIES* GROW BORED. THEY WILL CHARGE EARLY, AND THEY WILL *LOSE.*

YOU WILL PLAY YOUR PART. IT IS *GOD* WHO COMMANDS IT.

—SOB—

THY WILL BE DONE, LORD.

JEHANNE! WHAT HAVE YOU *DONE*? WHERE ARE YOU GOING?

BACK TO BAUDRICOURT, FATHER HUGO. I HAVE TO CHANGE HIS MIND. HE NEEDS TO *SEE THE TRUTH.*

MY TIME IS *RUNNING OUT.* THE VOICES TELL ME THAT THE DAUPHIN'S *SCOTTISH ALLIES* ARE ABOUT TO MAKE A *TERRIBLE MISTAKE* WHILE FIGHTING THE ENGLISH.

YOU CAN'T GO ALONE! AND WHERE'S YOUR *CLOAK*? IT'S JANUARY! YOU'LL CATCH YOUR DEATH IN THE COLD.

GOD'S LOVE WILL KEEP ME WARM, FATHER HUGO. AND AS FOR HAVING SOMEONE WITH ME...

...YOU'D BETTER RIDE *FASTER,* THEN!

COME ON! KEEP UP! YAAH!!

MAKE WAY! I HAVE *IMPORTANT NEWS!*

CAPTAIN! THERE HAS BEEN A *TERRIBLE BATTLE!*

YOU. INSIDE. *NOW.*

THE COUNT OF CLERMONT WAS *TOO SLOW* TO HELP HIS SCOTTISH ALLIES, AND THEY WERE CUT DOWN BY THE ENGLISH.

THE SCOTTISH ATTACKED TOO SOON. THE *ARTILLERY* HAD TO STOP. THE ENGLISH WON.

FOUR HUNDRED MEN HAVE BEEN KILLED OR WOUNDED. *SIR JOHN STEWART*, THE LEADER OF THE SCOTS, IS DEAD. DUNOIS, THE *BASTARD OF ORLÉANS*, IS INJURED.

HOW DID YOU KNOW THIS?

HOW AMAZING THAT THE ANGELS CAN TELL YOU OF SUCH THINGS WELL BEFORE THEY HAPPEN!

TRULY A *MIRACLE!*

OH, MY *FATHER* HELPED ME—BUT *NOT* THE ONE YOU'RE THINKING OF, FATHER HUGO!

YEARS OF STANDING BESIDE MY FATHER AS HE PLANNED THE VILLAGE'S DEFENCES HAS GIVEN ME A *TACTICAL KNOWLEDGE* THAT I USED WHEN READING BAUDRICOURT'S MAP.

I SIMPLY *GUESSED* THE OUTCOME DRAWING ON MY OWN EXPERIENCE.

YOU *LIED!*

I HAD FAITH IN MY ANSWER, FATHER. ISN'T THAT ENOUGH?

THE VOICES DIDN'T HELP ME. LET'S HOPE THEY ARE MORE *ILLUMINATING* BY THE TIME WE REACH CHINON.

PERHAPS THEY DIDN'T GIVE YOU ALL THE FACTS BECAUSE THEY KNEW YOU'D FIND THE ANSWER ELSEWHERE?

QUITE POSSIBLLY. PERHAPS I CAN COMPLETE THIS TASK *WITHOUT* FOLLOWING MY PATH TO THE END.

PERHAPS THERE *IS* A *FUTURE* FOR ME...

THE LORD DOES MOVE IN *MYSTERIOUS WAYS*, MY CHILD!

YOU CAN'T BE *SERIOUS*, CHARLES! A *LUNATIC CHILD* SENT BY BAUDRICOURT IS NOT THE ANSWER. YOUR COMMANDERS WOULD LAUGH YOU OFF THE *FIELD OF BATTLE* IF THEY HEARD OF THIS!

SHE'S POSSESSED BY *DEVILS*! DEVILS THAT CONVINCED HIM TO GIVE HER PASSAGE.

ROBERT IS A FINE JUDGE OF CHARACTER, MOTHER. IF HE SAYS THAT WE SHOULD *SPEAK* TO THIS GIRL, THEN WE SHOULD. WHAT HAVE WE GOT TO LOSE?

IF SHE TRULY IS BLESSED BY GOD—OR EVEN IF SHE IS TOUCHED WITH SEEING THE FUTURE—IT WOULD BE OF *GREAT AID* TO FRANCE!

MY LORD, THE GIRL IS HERE.

EXCELLENT. KEEP HER WAITING. I HAVE A PLAN...

PIERRE, COME, SIT ON THE THRONE. BE *ME* FOR A MOMENT.

MY LORD? I DON'T UNDERSTAND.

WHEN THE GIRL ENTERS, SHE WILL APPROACH *YOU*—FOR *YOU* WILL BE ON THE THRONE.

BUT, IF GOD *REALLY* SPEAKS TO HER—

HE WILL LET HER KNOW OF THE *DECEPTION*. IF SHE FINDS THE TRUE CHARLES, SHE IS *LESS* OF A FRAUD.

LET'S SEE HOW GOOD HER "VOICES" ARE!

MY LORD DAUPHIN. I ALMOST *MISSED* YOU IN THE CROWD.

INTERESTING ... SHE CERTAINLY FOUND YOU FAST ENOUGH! MAYBE SHE'S NOT AS MAD AS WE THOUGHT?

OR IT COULD HAVE BEEN TH— *HALF A DOZE PAINTINGS* C ME SHE PASSE TO REACH TH *VERY ROOM,* MOTHER!

I NEED MORE THAN THAT, I'M AFRAID!

IF YOU GIVE ME LEAVE TO SPEAK TO YOU *PRIVATELY,* MY LORD...

...I CAN OFFER YOU MORE. SOMETHING *ONLY YOU* KNOW.

EVERYONE AWAY! I WANT TO SEE THIS MAGIC TRICK.

COME ON! EVEN YOU, MOTHER.

YOU WORRY ABOUT YOUR *LEGITIMACY.* WHETHER YOU TRULY ARE YOUR *FATHER'S SON.*

MY FATHER TELLS YOU TO WORRY NO MORE. *YOU ARE HE.*

HOW DID—? *NOBODY* KNOWS THAT I HAVE WORRIED ABOUT THIS!

I DO NOT SEEK *GLORY*; I DO NOT DESIRE *RICHES*. I AM MORE THAN JUST A MESSENGER FROM GOD—I AM A *FIGHTER*, A *PATRIOT FOR FRANCE*, AND I HAVE TWO TASKS.

FIRST, TO LIFT THE SIEGE AT ORLÉANS, HELD THESE LAST FIVE MONTHS.

SECOND, TO LEAD THE DAUPHIN TO REIMS FOR HIS *CORONATION AND ANOINTING*.

GOD KNOWS, MY LIEGE.

REIMS? THAT'S UNDER *ENGLISH CONTROL*. IT'LL NEVER HAPPEN.

I'M THE *ARCHBISHOP* THERE, AND I'VE NOT SET FOOT IN MY CATHEDRAL FOR *YEARS*.

THEN I WILL HAVE TO WORK *HARDER* TO MAKE IT SO, WON'T I?

AND YOU WILL HELP, *RENAULT DE CHARTRES*, FOR GOD HAS *TOLD* ME ABOUT YOU. AFTER ALL, YOU WILL BE THE ONE WHO CROWNS THE KING!

I NEED TO DECIDE WHETHER THIS GIRL IS A *PROPHET* OR A *MADWOMAN* POSSESSED BY DEVILS.

CHANCELLOR, TAKE HER TO THE *NUNS AT POITIERS*. *EXAMINE* HER. TEST HER. MAKE YOUR DECISIONS. IF SHE SPEAKS FOR GOD, THEN WE CAN USE HER TO INSPIRE OUR SOLDIERS.

IF SHE FAILS, THEN SHE IS A *WITCH*. A *HERETIC*. AND SHE WILL *BURN*.

POITIERS. DAY ONE.

WE HAVE EXAMINED HER *THOROUGHLY*, SISTER.

SHE IS STILL A *VIRGIN*.

DAY TWO.

YOU CLAIM GOD WISHES TO *HELP* FRANCE, BUT WHY?

SURELY ENGLAND IS *LOVED BY GOD* TOO?

FRANCE HAS BEEN BROUGHT SO LOW THROUGH THESE YEARS OF ENDLESS BATTLE THAT GOD WILL TAKE *MERCY* ON US.

DO YOU EVEN *BELIEVE* IN GOD?

YES. BETTER THAN *YOU*.

DAY THREE.

WE CANNOT GIVE YOU SOLDIERS BASED SOLELY ON YOUR *ASSERTIONS!*

WE CANNOT SEND THEM INTO *DANGER* WITHOUT SOME SORT OF SIGN.

IN THE NAME OF GOD, I HAVE NOT COME TO POITIERS TO *GIVE SIGNS*.

TAKE ME TO ORLÉANS AND I WILL *SHOW YOU* SIGNS PROVING WHY I HAVE BEEN SENT.

SHE HAS SPIRIT, A SHARP WIT, AND CONFIDENCE.

SHE'LL MEASURE UP TO THE CHALLENGES AHEAD.

THE CHURCHMEN SAY SHE MAY *FULFIL* HER PROMISES.

THE FRENCH ARMIES ARE *CONSTANTLY* BEING BEATEN BY THE ENGLISH. OUR ALLIES ARE INCOMPETENT, AND MORALE IS SO LOW RIGHT NOW THAT *ANYTHING* SHE DOES CAN ONLY HELP US.

JOAN, YOU'VE IMPRESSED US ALL. WE TRULY BELIEVE THAT YOU HAVE THE *VOICE OF GOD* TO GUIDE YOU.

WITH YOUR HELP, WE CAN FINALLY REGAIN *ORLÉANS* — AND I CAN BE CROWNED *KING*.

I THEREFORE MAKE YOU, *JOAN D'ARC*, ONE OF MY KNIGHTS. AND WITH SUCH STANDING COMES A SWORD—

FORGIVE ME, SIRE, BUT THIS IS *NOT* THE SWORD I MUST TAKE.

I AM HERE TO LEAD, TO BE AN *EXAMPLE*, AND MY SWORD MUST BE A SYMBOL OF *EQUAL WORTH*.

I KNOW WHERE ONE SUCH SWORD LIES: BEHIND THE ALTAR IN THE *CHURCH OF SAINT CATHERINE OF FIERBOIS*.

IMPOSSIBLE! HOW CAN YOU BE CERTAIN THAT SUCH A SWORD EXISTS?

AND THAT IT WILL STILL BE THERE AFTER *SO MANY CENTURIES*?

OH, MY LORD, HAVEN'T YOU GUESSED?

SAINT CATHERINE HERSELF TOLD ME.

THE CHURCH OF SAINT CATHERINE OF FIERBOIS.

THE VOICES TOLD ME THE SWORD WOULD BE BEHIND THE ALTAR.

I KNOW YOU'RE THE *DUKE OF ALENÇON*, BUT COULD YOU *HELP* HERE?

OF COURSE, MY DEAR. AND PLEASE, CALL ME *JEAN*.

IT'S RUDE TO INSIST ON TITLES WITH A GIRL WHO SPEAKS WITH *GOD*, NO?

PUT YOUR BACKS INTO IT—*HNF*—!

THIS WEIGHS A TON! I HOPE YOU'RE CORRECT.

THERE'S NOTHING HERE! YOUR VOICES WERE *WRONG*!

DID YOU THINK IT WOULD SIMPLY BE *RESTING* THERE FOR ME?

SACRED OBJECTS SUCH AS THIS MUST BE FOUND. *EARNED*.

SHE NEEDS A BANNER PEOPLE CAN FOLLOW.

HOW ABOUT A PAINTING OF *GOD IN HEAVEN,* FLANKED BY ANGELS!

AND ADD THE WORDS *"JHESUS MARIA"!*

THAT'S IT, JOAN! HOLD THE REINS!

IN A BATTLE YOU *CAN'T* ALLOW THEM TO DISLODGE YOU FROM YOUR STEED. GOD CAN'T STOP YOU FALLING OFF A HORSE!

YOUR MEN ARE READY TO RIDE TO *ORLÉANS,* MA'AM.

MY DEAR DUKE.

JUST GIVE THE WORD AND WE'LL LEAVE.

MOUNT UP.

ORLÉANS.

WE'VE DESTROYED THE BRIDGE TO *LES TOURELLES*, IF WE CAN JUST WAIT IT OUT A LITTLE LONGER...

MORE THAN *SIX MONTHS* YOU'VE BEEN SAYING THIS, DUNOIS! THE PEOPLE OF ORLÉANS ARE *STARVING*!

WE'RE CONSTANTLY ATTACKED BY THE ENGLISH, AND OUR FOOD SUPPLIES TAKEN FOR THEIR *OWN SOLDIERS*. EVEN ALL THE *RATS* HAVE BEEN EATEN BY NOW!

WE'RE *ALL* STARVING! DO YOU SEE ANY FOOD HERE? *NO!*

WE'RE TRYING TO MAKE A DEAL WITH THE *BURGUNDIANS*; PERHAPS IF THEY AGREE AND STEP BACK, THERE WILL BE *FEWER SOLDIERS* TO FIGHT THROUGH!

AND, OF COURSE, THE DAUPHIN SENDS US THE *MAID*, THE MESSENGER FROM GOD, RATHER THAN SUPPLIES.

PRAISE BE TO HEAVEN. WE ARE SAVED!

WHAT DO YOU MEAN—*MAID*?

SPEAK CLEARER, GILLES!

HAVE YOU NOT HEARD? CHARLES SENDS *JOAN D'ARC*, A *PROPHET* WITH AN ARMY OF CLERGYMEN AND *ROYAL GUARD!*

SHE'S SUPPOSED TO END THE SIEGE. I JUST HOPE SHE BRINGS SOME *BREAD!*

TAKE COVER! THE ENGLISH ARE FIRING THE CATAPULTS AGAIN!

SHE SPEAKS TO GOD, THEY SAY. AND SHE WANTS THE ENGLISH GONE.

SHE'S ALREADY WRITTEN TWO LETTERS TO THE ENGLISH COMMANDER, TALBOT, TELLING HIM TO SURRENDER AND LEAVE!

WRITING LETTERS? TRULY THE WORK OF A WOMAN. STILL, IF SHE BRINGS US ANY SOLDIERS AND SUPPLIES, SHE'LL BE WELL RECEIVED.

A GIRL AS PERSISTENT AS THIS JOAN SOUNDS COULD BE GOOD FOR MORALE. ALREADY, THE TROOPS TALK ABOUT HER.

LET'S HOPE SHE ARRIVES SOON— WE MAY NEED HER PRAYERS QUICKER THAN SHE THINKS.

MY LORD, WHERE IS *TALBOT*? I SENT HERALDS AHEAD STATING THAT I WISHED TO SPEAK TO HIM.

WELL, WE'VE DESTROYED THE BRIDGE THAT WOULD HAVE TAKEN HIM, AND THERE'S NO WIND TO SAIL THE BARGES ACROSS.

SO I'M AFRAID *THAT'S* OUT OF THE QUESTION.

HOW *DARE* YOU COUNTERMAND MY ORDERS! WHY DID WE MEET ON *THIS* SIDE OF THE LOIRE?

WE COULD HAVE MET ON THE *OTHER* SIDE AND GONE TOGETHER TO SEE HIM!

AYE, AND BEEN *KILLED* TOGETHER! YOU MIGHT BE A MESSENGER FROM GOD, GIRL...

...BUT TO THE ENGLISH YOU'RE JUST A *WITCH WITH A BANNER!*

AT LEAST COME TO ORLÉANS AND REST BEFORE WE WORK OUT WHAT TO DO NEXT!

WHAT TO DO NEXT? WHY IS THAT DIFFICULT? WE *ATTACK!*

WE ATTACK LES TOURELLES *IMMEDIATELY!*

I WISH JOAN LUCK. SHE'S A FIREBRAND. AND SHE'LL GET HER OWN WAY.

I HAVE NO DOUBT.

SO, HOW LONG *DID* YOU WAIT BEHIND THE RIDGE UNTIL THE SUN SHONE?

I HAVE NO IDEA WHAT YOU MEAN, BROTHER.

...

ABOUT *TWO HOURS!*

HA-HA-HA!

THAT'S WHAT WE THINK OF YOUR OFFER TO LET US SURRENDER!

WHEN WE CAPTURE YOUR WITCH, WE'LL BURN HER!

THEY'RE FIRING FLAMING ARROWS AT US IN RESPONSE TO A MESSAGE YOU SENT!

WHAT DID YOU SAY?

I SIMPLY GAVE TALBOT ONE LAST CHANCE TO LEAVE! WHY ARE YOU SO ANGRY?

BECAUSE YOU'VE STIRRED THEM UP, YOU FOOL!

THEY WANT A FIGHT, AND NOW WE'LL HAVE TO GIVE IT TO THEM.

GOOD! WE NEED TO ATTACK. WE START TOMORROW.

LOVED BY GOD OR NOT, I SWEAR I WILL PUT AN ARROW IN HER MYSELF!

WE SET OFF TOMORROW MORNING, BUT NOT WITH HER.

THEN THE FOOL WILL LOSE THE BATTLE.

I HAVE TO GET THERE BEFORE HE *RUINS* EVERYTHING!

...HE WALLS OF LES TOURELLES.

IT'S *NO USE!* THERE ARE *TOO MANY* OF THEM. OUR LINES ARE BREAKING! OUR SOLDIERS ARE FLEEING.

WE SHOULD HAVE BROUGHT THE GIRL AND HER CLERICS— THEY COULD AT LEAST HAVE GIVEN US *LAST RITES!*

WE WERE *SO CLOSE.*

SOUND THE RETREAT!

LOOK! WE'RE SAVED!

MY LORD, I FEAR IT IS A **MORTAL** WOUND! I'VE SEEN MEN DIE FROM FAR LESS.

THE BEST I CAN DO IS MAKE HER **COMFORTABLE**— SHE WON'T LAST THE DAY!

I CAN'T... HEAR... WHAT DID... HE SAY...?

YOU NEED TO REST, JOAN. HERE, TAKE THIS...

...IT'S AN **OPIATE**— A DRUG THAT WILL **NUMB** ALL PAIN.

NO... NEED CLEAR HEAD... FOR FIGHTING...

THERE'S NO MORE FIGHTING FOR **YOU**, DEAR GIRL.

JUST **GLORY** AT THE LORD'S SIDE.

STOP... STANDING AROUND... GO ...FIGHT...

...

SHE'S GONE.

THE MAID OF ORLÉANS IS DEAD.

CHINON.

MY LORD DAUPHIN, I BRING NEWS FROM ORLÉANS.

JOAN HAS **BROKEN THE SIEGE!** THE ENGLISH HAVE SURRENDERED THE CITY!

I **KNEW** THAT SENDING HER WOULD BE A BLESSING! WITH HER TO INSPIRE THE TROOPS, AND WITH MEN LIKE THE BASTARD, GILLES, JEAN...

WE COULD WIN BACK ALL OF FRANCE!

PARIS SHOULD BE NEXT—IT'S CLOSE TO ORLÉANS. THEY CAN **REST** BEFORE THEY MOVE ON—

OH, NO, MA'AM! THEY'VE ALREADY MOVED ON!

THEY MARCH TO **JARGEAU!** JOAN AIMS TO CLEAR THE **LOIRE VALLEY** OF ALL ENGLISH GARRISONS.

AND WHEN THAT TASK IS COMPLETE, THEY HEAD FOR **REIMS!**

REIMS? THAT'S **TWICE** AS FAR AS PARIS!

AND AS THEY MARCH, THE ENGLISH WILL HAVE TIME TO SUMMON REINFORCEMENTS!

SHE'S DOING WHAT SHE SWORE SHE WOULD, MOTHER. SHE'S ENSURING THAT I WILL BE CROWNED AT REIMS.

THE **MAID OF ORLÉANS** IS MORE THAN JUST A SIMPLE PEASANT GIRL NOW—SHE IS A **MIRACLE** WORKER.

LET US LEAVE HER TO CREATE **MORE** MIRACLES FOR FRANCE.

WITH THE BRIDGE AT ORLÉANS *DESTROYED*, AND THE OTHER CROSSINGS LOST, THIS IS THE *ONLY ROUTE* NORTH OF THE RIVER.

THERE ARE THREE MAIN AREAS: THE *BRIDGE FORTIFICATION*, THE *CITY*, AND THE *CASTLE* ON THE EDGE.

WE DON'T HAVE THE MANPOWER TO CONDUCT A SIEGE, JOAN. AND THE CASTLE WILL BE A NIGHTMARE TO BREAK DOWN.

IT WOULD STOP THE ENGLISH FROM REACHING THE *SOUTH OF FRANCE*, THOUGH.

TRUE. BUT AT WHAT COST?

THE PROBLEM WITH YOU, GENTLEMEN, IS THAT YOU THINK LIKE *KNIGHTS*. LIKE *LORDS*.

I GREW UP LEARNING STRATEGY FROM A *VILLAGE MILITIA*. WE ALWAYS LOOKED AT THE *SMALLER* PICTURE.

THE CITY *SURVIVES* BY FORAGING SOUTH OF THE RIVER, RIGHT?

THEN WE SIMPLY TAKE THE BRIDGE. INSTALL A GARRISON. *STOP* THE ENGLISH.

NO FOOD— NO FIGHT.

MY GOD, IT'S SO *SIMPLE*! WE COULD DO IT TONIGHT!

THEN *DO* IT TONIGHT. AND SET UP CANNON TO BLAST ACROSS THE LOIRE AT THE CASTLE.

WE CAN'T LET THE ENGLISH SOLDIERS FEEL *FORGOTTEN*, NOW, CAN WE?

MY **LORD TALBOT**, YOU SEEM TO KEEP **LOSING TO A GIRL**.

ORLÉANS, JARGEAU, MEUNG-SUR-LOIRE, AND NOW **BEAUGENCY.**

I HAD NO CHOICE AT BEAUGENCY, SIR JOHN. WE HEARD OF ANOTHER **THOUSAND** TROOPS ARRIVING, LED BY **ARTHUR DE RICHEMONT.**

WE FELT IT MORE... **PRUDENT** TO JOIN WITH YOU.

FOUR ENGLISH GARRISONS! **FOUR!**

ALL LOST TO A WITCH OF A CHILD! WHAT **DEVILRY** DOES SHE USE?

A MORTAL WOUND FROM AN ARROW, A SKULL CRUSHED BY A BOULDER...

...SHRUGGED OFF LIKE A **STING FROM A HORNET!** WHAT MANNER OF WOMAN IS THIS?

SHE'S AN **INSPIRATION**, SIR JOHN. AND BY THAT I MEAN SHE INSPIRES THE FRENCH TO FIGHT **HARDER** THAN THEY EVER HAVE BEFORE.

THEY'VE TAKEN **EVERY FORT THEY'VE FACED** SINCE SHE ARRIVED—

THEN WE **STOP GIVING HER FORTS TO CAPTURE.** WE FIGHT THEM ON **OPEN GROUND,** LIKE WE ALWAYS HAVE.

PREPARE YOUR MEN, TALBOT. WE MARCH TO WAR...

...WE MAKE OUR STAND AT **PATAY.**

IT SEEMS I OWE YOU A CROWN AND A COUNTRY, JOAN. YOUR PROPHECIES *BOTH* CAME TO PASS.

SO WHAT NEXT?

YOUR MAJESTY, I'D LIKE TO CONTINUE TO *PARIS.* I BELIEVE WE CAN HAVE THE ENGLISH OUT WITHIN *SEVEN YEARS...*

...BUT I'D LIKE TO TRY *BEFORE* THAT.

GO TO PARIS. BUILD YOUR TROOPS. BUT, AS THE ANOINTED KING NOW, I MUST TRY *DIPLOMACY* FIRST.

IF THAT FAILS, THEN I WILL GIVE YOU *ALL THE ASSISTANCE YOU NEED.*

THANK YOU, MY LIEGE.

JOAN, BEFORE YOU LEAVE... THAT BANNER.

WHY *DID* YOU HOLD IT AT MY CORONATION?

IT BORE THE *BURDEN* OF BATTLE. IT WAS QUITE RIGHT THAT IT SHOULD RECEIVE THE *HONOUR* TOO.

SEND YOUR DIPLOMATS, MY KING. I'LL PREPARE MY *ARMY.*

8 SEPTEMBER. THE ASSAULT ON PARIS.

AND YET STILL I HEAR THE *LORD'S VOICE* TELLING ME TO CONTINUE—

MY SWORD! I FORGOT TO BRING SAINT CATHERINE'S SWORD!

I TELL YOU, JEAN, NOW HE'S KING, CHARLES DOESN'T SEEM *INTERESTED* IN WAR!

HIS DIPLOMATS FAILED, SO WHERE ARE THE *TROOPS* HE PROMISED US?

WHY DO *YOU* CARE, JOAN? YOUR JOB IS DONE. YOU HAD TWO TASKS TO FULFIL...

...FREE ORLÉANS AND CROWN CHARLES! *GO HOME! HAVE A FAMILY.*

HERE, TAKE *THIS* ONE. HE DOESN'T HAVE NEED OF IT ANY MORE!

LOOK OUT— *ARGH!*

JOAN? THE CONVOY IS LEAVING. WE NEED TO GET MOVING.

I KNOW, I JUST NEEDED TO BE ALONE FOR A MOMENT.

I THOUGHT OF ALL OF US, YOU WERE THE ONE WHO WAS NEVER ALONE.

IS THIS THE SWORD I FOUND FOR YOU? YOU'RE LEAVING IT HERE?

IT'S CUSTOMARY TO LEAVE AN OFFERING. I FELT IT WAS A WORTHY ONE.

AFTER ALL, THE KING DOESN'T THINK ME WORTHY ENOUGH TO WIELD IT.

GO BACK TO YOUR WIFE, JEAN. BE WITH HER THIS WINTER. FOR, IN SPRING, THIS TRUCE WILL FALL...

...AND I WILL BE AT WAR AGAIN. MY TRUE SWORD WILL BE UNSHEATHED ONCE MORE.

HOW DO YOU KNOW THIS? THE VOICES? GOD HIMSELF?

WHAT HAS HE SAID?

THE SAME AS HE ALWAYS DOES. THAT I WILL BE CAPTURED BY THE ENGLISH BEFORE MIDSUMMER...

...AND DEAD WITHIN TWO YEARS.

AUTUMN. BOURGES.

MY LORD, WHY HAVE YOU *FORSAKEN* ME?

WHY WON'T YOU SPEAK?

LOIRE.

THIS TREATY IS GOOD FOR *BOTH* SIDES. FOR IF FRANCE AND BURGUNDY CONTINUE THIS ALLIANCE...

...THEN THE ENGLISH CAN *NEVER* WIN.

WINTER.

SO THE KING MADE YOU A *NOBLEWOMAN*? THAT IS A FINE REWARD.

DO YOU STILL HEAR THE VOICES?

NO, FATHER, NOT FOR MANY MONTHS NOW.

I KNOW THAT THIS TREATY IS *WRONG*. THE BURGUNDIANS WILL ALLY THEMSELVES AGAIN WITH THE ENGLISH.

BUT THE KING WILL NOT *LISTEN* TO ME. HE GIVES ME *TITLES* INSTEAD OF *SOLDIERS*.

HE SAYS DIPLOMACY IS *CHEAPER* THAN WAR.

BUT HE STILL BLAMES ME FOR *PARIS*. HE STILL BLAMES ME FOR FAILING.

AND *SO* DOES GOD.

SPRING. 1430.

BLESS ME, FATHER, FOR I HAVE—

WHY ARE YOU *HERE*, JOAN? *WHY DO YOU NOT FIGHT?*

MY LORD BEDFORD, I HAVE NEWS!

GO ON, THEN! OUT WITH IT, LAD!

THE WOMAN—JOAN THE MAID—SHE'S BEEN *CAPTURED*!

THEY TOOK HER AT COMPIÈGNE!

EXCELLENT! CALL THE PRIESTS. I WANT THEM TO DRAW UP *CHARGES OF HERESY*!

CONTACT HER GAOLERS. ASK THEM HOW MUCH THEY *WANT* FOR THE WITCH!

LORD BEDFORD! SHE'S A *CHILD*!

SHE'S NOT A CHILD, WALLACE. SHE'S A *MILITARY COMMANDER*. SO TREAT HER LIKE ONE.

CHARLES STAGED HIS *CORONATION* ON THE BACK OF HER VISIONS. IF SHE IS DISCREDITED, THEN *SO IS HE*.

BUT STILL, THE KING SHOULD BE MADE AWARE—

THE KING IS CURRENTLY AN *EIGHT-YEAR-OLD BOY* WHO DOESN'T EVEN KNOW *WHY HE IS IN FRANCE*!

WE WILL BUY THE MAID OF ORLÉANS, AND WE WILL TRY HER. DISCREDIT HER.

AND THEN WE WILL *BURN* HER.

OCTOBER 1430. THE FORTRESS OF BEAUREVOIR.

FOOD FOR YOU ... LADY JEANNE SAID WE HAD TO TREAT YOU PROPERLY.

SO HOW ABOUT YOU *RETURN THE FAVOUR* AND TAKE OFF THAT STUPID UNIFORM? WE HAVE PLENTY OF LOVELY *DRESSES* YOU COULD WEAR!

THANK YOU, BUT I CANNOT.

GOD HASN'T GIVEN ME *LEAVE* TO CHANGE MY CLOTHES.

YOUR DECISION. BUT IT MIGHT BE *TAKEN* FROM YOU SOON. I HEARD BURGUNDY'S NEGOTIATING WITH THE *ENGLISH*.

THEY'RE OFFERING A *LOT OF MONEY* FOR YOU.

BUT THAT ISN'T HOW RANSOMS WORK! FRANCE PAYS THE RANSOM!

I DON'T GET SOLD TO A *BETTER BUYER!*

THE ENGLISH DON'T WANT YOU TAKING THE FIELD AGAIN.

AND THEIR POCKET IS *BIGGER* THAN YOUR KING'S.

I WILL NOT BE SOLD TO THE ENGLISH!

I'D RATHER DIE THAN BE SOLD TO THE ENGLISH!

I'D RATHER DIE.

CHINON.

APPARENTLY JOAN WAS INJURED WHILE TRYING TO *ESCAPE*. ALTHOUGH FALLING SIXTY FEET OFF A BALCONY SOUNDS MORE LIKE A *SUICIDE ATTEMPT*.

BECAUSE OF THIS, LIGNY HAS *ACCEPTED* THE ENGLISH OFFER OF *TEN THOUSAND GOLD CROWNS* FOR HER.

WE *CAN'T* LET THAT *HAPPEN*, YOUR MAJESTY!

DO YOU THINK I *WANT* IT TO? WE *DON'T HAVE* TEN THOUSAND GOLD CROWNS! WE'RE BARELY HOLDING ON HERE!

WE CAN'T RAISE AN ARMY OVER ONE GIRL— EVEN *THIS* GIRL! MY CROWN TEETERS ON A *KNIFE EDGE* AT THE MOMENT!

THEN WHY *CALL ME HERE*, SIRE?

BECAUSE THERE ARE *OTHER* WAYS TO FIGHT THIS. THE ENGLISH WANT TO TRY JOAN FOR *HERESY*.

IF JOAN IS BRANDED A *WITCH*, AND I TOOK *ADVICE* FROM HER? I'D LOSE THE BACKING OF THE CHURCH.

IT WOULD WEAKEN MY HOLD ON FRANCE, AND MAKE THE CLAIM OF ENGLAND'S HENRY STRONGER.

AND THE ENGLISH WOULD *OWN* HIM.

THEY WISH TO HOLD THE TRIAL IN *ROUEN*, BUT HAVE AGREED TO HAVE AS MANY FRENCH CLERGY AS ENGLISH THERE.

OFFICIALLY THEY'LL BE THERE FOR THE SAME REASON— THE CHARGE OF *HERESY*. BUT UNOFFICIALLY? THEY'LL BE TRYING TO FIND A *LOOPHOLE* TO FREE JOAN.

I WANT YOU TO ACCOMPANY THE *DOMINICAN YSAMBARD DE LA PIERRE* THERE. I WANT YOU TO BE A COMFORT TO JOAN. TELL HER...

...TELL HER I WISH I COULD HAVE *DONE MORE*.

TELL HER IT'S IN *GOD'S* HANDS NOW.

MARCH.

YOU DICTATED LETTERS: DURING *YOUR LOIRE* CAMPAIGN, AM I RIGHT?

ONE STATED "BEFORE *SEVEN YEARS* ARE PAST THE ENGLISH WILL LOSE A GREATER STAKE THAN THEY DID AT ORLÉANS, FOR THEY WILL LOSE *EVERYTHING IN FRANCE.*"

HOW DO YOU KNOW THIS? AND WHAT DOES IT MEAN?

IT MEANS WHAT IT STATES. IN LESS THAN SEVEN YEARS *PARIS* WILL FALL. THE ENGLISH WILL LOSE *EVERYTHING* IN FRANCE.

HOW DO I KNOW? *GOD* HAS TOLD ME.

YOUR APPARITIONS... WERE THEY MALE? FEMALE? DID THEY HAVE HAIR?

SAINT MARGARET— DIDN'T SHE SPEAK ENGLISH?

WHY SHOULD SHE SPEAK ENGLISH WHEN SHE ISN'T ON THE *ENGLISH* SIDE?

YOU MENTION A *SIGN* THAT YOU GAVE TO THE KING, SO THAT HE WOULD KNOW THE TRUTH OF YOUR WORDS.

WHAT WAS THAT SIGN?

GO AND ASK *HIM.*

YOU ALSO MET WITH *CATHERINE DE LA ROCHELLE*, A FRENCH MYSTIC WHO *ALSO* CLAIMS TO HAVE REVELATIONS FROM GOD.

SHE IS *NOTHING*— A FOLLY AND NOTHING MORE.

MY SAINTS TOLD ME SO.

WHILE YOU WERE AT *BEAUREVOIR*, YOU LEAPED SIXTY FEET FROM A BALCONY. YOU WERE BADLY INJURED...

...BUT WERE YOU TRYING TO ESCAPE OR *KILL* YOURSELF?

I LEAPED FROM FEAR OF THE ENGLISH, AND COMMENDED MYSELF TO GOD...

...FOR I WOULD RATHER *SURRENDER MY SOUL TO GOD* THAN FALL INTO THE HANDS OF THE ENGLISH.

I DON'T THINK THE GIRL *LIKES YOU*, MY LORD WARWICK.

SHE'LL LIKE ME EVEN *LESS* WHEN I *BURN HER.*

THIS FARCE IS *OVER* FOR THE DAY.

CAUCHON? I WOULD HAVE *WORDS* WITH YOU.

THE EARL OF WARWICK'S CHAMBERS.

WHOSE SIDE ARE YOU ON, CAUCHON?

WHY, THE CHURCH'S SIDE, MY LORD WARWICK.

WRONG. YOU'RE ON OUR SIDE, WHETHER YOU LIKE IT OR NOT.

ROUEN IS IN ENGLISH HANDS. WE ALLOW YOU TO PRESIDE OVER THIS TRIAL OUT OF THE GOODNESS OF OUR HEARTS.

IF YOU CARRY ON LIKE THIS, IT WON'T TAKE MUCH TO REMOVE YOU, AND FIND SOMEONE MORE SUITED TO THE TASK!

BUT, MY LORD...THE HOLY ROMAN CHURCH...

THE POPE? IS HE HERE? UNDER THESE, PERHAPS? NO?

THE POPE BE DAMNED. HE'S NOT HERE. I AM. AND SO IS A GARRISON OF ENGLISH SOLDIERS WHO ALL WANT THAT WITCH DEAD.

DON'T DISAPPOINT US, BISHOP.

LET'S JUST SAY THAT YOUR SPIRITUAL FUTURE DEPENDS ON IT.

23 MAY 1431.

SHE TWISTS OUR STATEMENTS AT EVERY TURN AND ANSWERS A QUESTION WITH ANOTHER...

DO YOU HAVE A *VERDICT*? WHEN DO WE BURN HER?

IT'S NOT YET DECIDED IF SHE *IS* TO BE BURNED, MY LORD WARWICK. THE CHURCH HAS STRICT GUIDELINES—

TO HELL WITH YOUR GUIDELINES! I WANT HER BURNT TOMORROW!

MY LORD! IF YOU WANT HER TRIED BY THE CHURCH, THEN YOU HAVE TO *ABIDE BY OUR RULES!* UNLESS SHE *REFUSES TO RECANT* HER HERESY, SHE CANNOT BE BURNT.

IF YOU WANT ANOTHER VERDICT, THEN *TRY HER YOURSELF!*

MY MEN WILL NOT *FIGHT* UNTIL THEY KNOW THAT SHE IS *DEAD!*

FOR *MONTHS* YOU HAVE SAT AROUND THAT TABLE DOING *NOTHING.* WHY ARE YOU SCARED OF A *GIRL*?

IT'S NOT THE *GIRL* WE'RE SCARED OF; IT'S THE *VOICES.*

IF THEY'RE REAL, THEN WE ARE *ARGUING AGAINST GOD.* AND TO DO THAT IS TRULY THE WAY TO *DAMN YOUR SOUL.*

24 MAY.

FRANCE, THE BASTION OF TRUE CHRISTIANITY, MUST WEEP, FOR IT HAS BEEN ABUSED!

CHARLES, WHO CALLS HIMSELF *KING*, HAS FOLLOWED THE WORDS OF THIS *WORTHLESS WOMAN*, WHO IS FULL OF DISHONOUR!

I DENOUNCE YOU FOR HERESY!

BY MY FAITH, SIR, THERE IS NO *NOBLER CHRISTIAN TO BE FOUND* THAN THE KING.

SHAME ON YOU, FOR THE KING IS NOT LIKE YOU SAY. HE *LOVES* THE FAITH AND THE CHURCH.

WHY IS MY TRIAL NOT HEARD BY *ROME*? WHY DOES THE *POPE* NOT MAKE THE FINAL DECISION?

BECAUSE ROME IS *TOO FAR AWAY*! BAILIFF! PLEASE, SILENCE HER!

BUT ONE OF MY CHARGES WAS THAT I *REFUSED TO SUBMIT TO THE HOLY CHURCH OF ROME.*

IF I AM NOT *ABLE* TO FACE THEM, HOW CAN I *REFUSE*?

THE LIST GOES ON. BUT THE CHURCH IS MERCIFUL. *RECANT YOUR SINS*, JOAN. APOLOGIZE.

YOU ARE GUILTY OF *SO MANY SINS*. FIRST, THAT YOU *WORE AND STILL WEAR MEN'S CLOTHES* AND YOUR HAIR *SHORT*, CLAIMING THAT GOD COMMANDED YOU SO.

YOU PRETENDED TO HAVE HAD *REVELATIONS AND APPARITIONS OF GOD, THE ANGELS, SAINT CATHERINE, AND SAINT MARGARET*.

YOU BORE ARMS IN BATTLE, *CRUELLY DESIRING HUMAN BLOOD*.

YOU HAVE *DESPISED GOD AND HIS SACRAMENTS*, ADORED AND INVOKED *EVIL SPIRITS*.

REFUSE TO WEAR THESE CLOTHES AGAIN. *RENOUNCE HERESY* AND MAKE SUITABLE PENANCE...

...AND THE CHURCH WILL WELCOME YOU BACK INTO ITS BOSOM.

IF YOU SIGN THIS, THEY *CANNOT* BURN YOU. THE ENGLISH AND BURGUNDIANS *CANNOT KEEP* YOU.

YOU WILL BE *FREE*, JOAN, AS LONG AS YOU REPENT.

BUT WHAT OF MY VOICES?

ASK THEM. DO *THEY* TELL YOU NOT TO SIGN?

IF YOU DO NOT DO THIS, CHILD, THERE IS EVERY POSSIBILITY THAT THE ENGLISH WILL *BURN YOU RIGHT NOW*.

I DON'T KNOW HOW TO READ OR WRITE. IS THIS *MARK* ACCEPTABLE?

VERY.

YOU HAVE *RETURNED TO THE CHURCH*, CHILD. BUT YOU MUST PAY FOR YOUR CRIMES.

THE PENANCE IS *PERPETUAL IMPRISONMENT*.

WHAT? YOU SAID SHE WOULD *GO FREE*!

CAUCHON! YOU LIED! YOU BORE FALSE WITNESS!

YOU'LL BURN IN HELL!

MY CHILD, HOW DID IT COME TO THIS?

HOW DID YOU *FALL* SO FAR?

THEY *TRICKED* ME—TORE MY CLOTHES OFF AND TOLD ME I WAS *DAMNED*.

WHAT DID YOU *THINK* I WOULD DO? I'M A *SOLDIER*!

NO, JOAN, YOU'RE JUST A GIRL.

A GIRL WITH AN *INCREDIBLE GIFT*, WHO HELPED FRANCE...

...BUT JUST A GIRL, STILL.

THEY'RE READYING THE PYRE AS WE SPEAK, JOAN. AT *TEN O'CLOCK* THIS MORNING THEY WILL TAKE YOU AND *EXECUTE* YOU.

AND THERE'S *NOTHING* I CAN DO TO STOP IT.

LET THEM BURN ME. I'VE KNOWN OF THIS FATE FOR *YEARS*. EVER SINCE ORLÉANS AND THE ARROW.

IT'S NOT MY *PHYSICAL SELF* I'M WORRIED ABOUT, BISHOP CAUCHON...

...IT'S MY *SPIRITUAL SELF*.

I CAN'T GO TO THE PYRE WITHOUT *CONFESSION*, FATHER! I JUST CAN'T!

WOULD YOU *DAMN MY SOUL AND LEAVE ME TO THE ENGLISH*?

NO, MY CHILD. THE CHURCH WOULD *NEVER* DO THAT.

FATHER HUGO WILL HEAR YOUR FINAL CONFESSION.

THANK YOU, FATHER. I FEEL BETTER KNOWING THAT MY SOUL IS SAVED.

IT'LL BE A *COMFORT* WHEN I'M IN THE FLAMES.

JOAN, REMEMBER ORLÉANS? WHEN YOU HAD THE *ARROW* IN YOU?

I OFFERED YOU A *DRUG* — ONE THAT WOULD NUMB YOU FOR HOURS, *STOP ALL PAIN*. I COULD GIVE THAT TO YOU...

NO, FATHER, I COULD NEVER *WILLINGLY* TAKE SOMETHING LIKE THAT.

IT WOULD *LESSEN* MY SACRIFICE TO GOD.

I UNDERSTAND, MY CHILD.

THEN LET US HAVE ONE FINAL *DRINK* TOGETHER AS WE WAIT FOR THE SUN TO RISE. THE BISHOP PROVIDED SOME *WINE* FOR US.

I'VE KNOWN YOU ALL YOUR LIFE, CHILD. IT FEELS *WRONG* TO STAND HERE AT THE END.

THANK YOU, FATHER, FOR BEING THERE WITH ME. FOR ALWAYS BELIEVING IN ME.

OH, I'VE ALWAYS BEEN THERE, JOAN. FOLLOWING YOU, ADVISING YOU...

... *PROTECTING* YOU.

FORGIVE ME, LORD, BUT I *WILL NOT LET HER SUFFER*.

30 MAY. THE EXECUTION OF JOAN OF ARC.

DO YOU HAVE ANY FINAL WORDS OR REQUESTS?

YES. I CALL UPON THE *FATHER, SON, AND THE HOLY SPIRIT.* I CALL UPON THE *BLESSED VIRGIN MARY* AND ALL THE SAINTS OF PARADISE.

PARDON MY JUDGES AND MY EXECUTIONER, FOR THEY *KNOW NOT* WHAT THEY DO.

I ASKED FOR A *CROSS* TO BE BROUGHT FROM SAINT SAUVEUR, SO I CAN SEE IT AS I END MY LIFE.

IS IT HERE?

YES, MY LADY. AND OR WHAT IT'S WORTH...

...I'M *SORRY*.

DO YOUR *DUTY*.

LORD, LET THE *MEDICINE WORK*. LET HER BE *NUMB* FROM ALL PAIN.

IN THE NAME OF *JESUS*!

MICHAEL! YOU COME TO ME!

IT IS TIME TO *COME HOME*, CHILD. TO SIT AT THE SIDE OF THE LORD, *BASKING IN HIS GLORY*.

THIS TIME HAS BEEN WELL KNOWN AND *PREPARED FOR*. WHILE THE FLAMES TAKE THIS MOST *MORTAL* OF BODIES...

HERE, FATHER—HER **ASHES**. THEY'RE TO BE SCATTERED OVER THE **SEINE**.

BUT THEY AGREED THAT **YOU** COULD DO IT IF YOU SO WISHED. AND WITH WHOMEVER YOU WANTED.

THANK YOU.

VEN LATER.

THANK YOU FOR COMING; IT WOULD HAVE MEANT A LOT TO HER.

I CAN'T STAY LONG—BEING A **MARSHAL OF FRANCE** IS A VERY DEMANDING ROLE. BUT, FOR JOAN...

IT WAS THE **LEAST** I COULD DO. ORLÉANS OWES **EVERYTHING** TO HER.

ALL I HAVE TO GO BACK TO IS MORE FIGHTING IN NORMANDY.

I **ASKED** FOR HER, YOU KNOW. I WROTE TO CHARLES AND ASKED HIM TO SEND JOAN TO HELP ME.

IF I'D TRIED HARDER, SHE MIGHT HAVE **SURVIVED**.

DID NONE OF HER **FAMILY** WISH TO BE HERE?

NO, HER FATHER IS ILL IN DOMRÉMY. BESIDES, **YOU** WERE HER FAMILY WHEN IT MATTERED.

AND DON'T CHASTISE YOURSELF SO, JEAN. SHE **ALWAYS** KNEW THAT THIS WAS TO BE HER FATE.

"IN THE SWEAT OF THY FACE SHALT THOU EAT BREAD, TILL THOU RETURN UNTO THE GROUND; FOR OUT OF IT WAST THOU TAKEN..."

"...AND UNTO **DUST** SHALT THOU RETURN."

GOOD-BYE, JEHANNE.

16 DECEMBER 1431.
CHINON.

THE ENGLISH CROWNED HENRY *KING OF FRANCE* TODAY, JOAN.

THEY THINK *THIS* GIVES HIM LEGITIMACY OVER ME. THEY *IGNORE* MY CLAIM.

I SHOULD HAVE *LISTENED* TO YOU. IF I'D FOUND THE TROOPS, PERHAPS PARIS *WOULD* HAVE FALLEN.

PERHAPS THINGS WOULD HAVE BEEN *DIFFERENT.*

PERHAPS YOU'D STILL BE *ALIVE.*

I'M SO *SORRY,* JOAN...

YOU *NEVER* HAVE TO APOLOGIZE TO ME, MY KING.

WE ALL HAD OUR *PARTS TO PLAY.*

IN 1435 CHARLES MADE A *TREATY* WITH THE BURGUNDIANS, BREAKING ENGLAND'S HOLD ON FRANCE FOREVER.

TWO YEARS LATER, HE *RECAPTURED* PARIS FROM THE ENGLISH—IN HONOUR OF JOAN.

IN 1449 HE REGAINED ROUEN AND THE FOLLOWING YEAR, WITH THE TRIAL RECORDS NOW HIS, DEMANDED A *RETRIAL* OF JOAN TO CLEAR HER NAME.

IN 1456 THE ORIGINAL VERDICT OF 1431 WAS *OVERTURNED* BY THE CHURCH, AND JOAN BECAME SEEN AS A MARTYR.

AFTER A *BEATIFICATION* IN 1909, JOAN OF ARC WAS MADE A *SAINT* IN 1920 BY *POPE BENEDICT XV*.

SAINT JOAN IS NOW A *PATRON SAINT OF FRANCE*, THE COUNTRY SHE *FOUGHT*, *SAVED*, AND *DIED* FOR.

THE END.

TONY LEE

Tony Lee has written for many popular comic books, including
X-Men, *Doctor Who*, *Spider-Man*, *Starship Troopers*,
Wallace & Gromit, and *Shrek*. His adaptation of
Pride & Prejudice & Zombies: The Graphic Novel was a
New York Times bestseller. He is also the author of the young
adult graphic novels *Outlaw: The Legend of Robin Hood* and
Excalibur: The Legend of King Arthur. Tony Lee lives in London.

SAM HART

Sam Hart is a comic book artist and magazine illustrator
who has worked on *Starship Troopers*, *Judge Dredd*,
and *Brothers: The Fall of Lucifer*. He is the illustrator
of Tony Lee's *Outlaw: The Legend of Robin Hood* and
Excalibur: The Legend of King Arthur. Born in England,
Sam Hart now lives and teaches comic art in Brazil.

STRONG BACK
OPEN FRONT

Sam Hart . 2011
AFTER
GERALDINE FARRA

Text copyright © 2014 by Tony Lee
Illustrations copyright © 2014 by Sam Hart

First U.S. edition 2015

Library of Congress Catalog Card Number 2013957283
ISBN 978-0-7636-7613-1 (hardcover)
ISBN 978-0-7636-7614-8 (paperback)

SWT 20 19 18 17 16 15
10 9 8 7 6 5 4 3 2 1

Printed in Dongguan, Guangdong, China

This book was typeset in CCWildWords.
The illustrations were created digitally.

Candlewick Press
99 Dover Street
Somerville, Massachusetts 02144

visit us at www.candlewick.com

To Tracy, my Muse and Inspiration.
And Doreen Lee, the first
and best editor I ever had.
Rest in Peace, Mum.

T. L.

For Kaya — grow strong,
little warrior.

S. H.

ACKNOWLEDGMENTS

With my loving thanks to many friends, among them:
Sasha Hart, Juliana Taioli and Lucas Taioli Hart,
Tamara Katzenstein, Suzana Katzenstein, Miriam Markus,
Daniel Markus, Elia Fernaldes, Frances Hollis, Flavio Luiz,
Eduardo and Manoela Schaal, Susana Salomão, Eduardo Gomes,
Sylvio Mello, Antonio Americo, Marcelo Campos, Igor Pessoa,
Mauricio Mudrik, Bia Cortese and Luiza Mudrik, Carlos Livieres,
Carol Lefevre, Sheila Finger, Octavio Cariello, Gualberto Costa
and Daniela Baptista, Rodrigo Reis, Soraya Lucato, Mario Colombo,
Jan Rocha, and Lise Forell.

S. H.